MIKE MAIHAC

CLEOPATRA
IN SPACE

BOOK FOUR
THE GOLDEN LION

AN IMPRINT OF

📖 SCHOLASTIC

Library of Congress Control Number: 2016944743

ISBN 978-0-545-83871-9 (hardcover)
ISBN 978-0-545-83872-6 (paperback)

10 9 8 7 6 5 4 3 2 1   17 18 19 20 21

Printed in China   38
First edition, July 2017
Color flatting by Dan Conner and Kate Carleton
Edited by Cassandra Pelham
Book design by Phil Falco
Creative Director: David Saylor

SCRAPE
SCRITCH

FLASH

CHAPTER ONE

OCTAVIAN.

BOOP

VRRRAK

VRRRAK

frizz

VRk

frizz

NOT YOU, TOO.

friz

I HAD THAT COVERED.

DUST DUST

VRRRR

VRRRR-CHACK

VRRRR

THOUGHT YOU COULD USE A *HAND*.

HAR HAR.

YOU'VE BEEN SPENDING A LOT OF TIME IN HERE LATELY.

EVEN FOR YOU.

ANYWAY, BIOLOGY IS IN FIVE MINUTES SO WE BETTER--

RESET SIMULATOR PROGRAM.

LEVEL TWELVE.

VRRRUMM

END SIMULATOR PROGRAM.

AW.

VRRRUMM

I THOUGHT YOU WEREN'T SKIPPING CLASSES ANYMORE?

UGH. I KNOOOOW.

WHY DOES BIOLOGY HAVE TO BE SO BORING?

BORING? WE LEARN ABOUT THE ENDOCRINE SYSTEM OF A TAWRISIAN TOAD TODAY!

YOU CALL THAT BORING?

34

YOU WERE GLOWING AGAIN.

I KNOW.

KHENSU'S BEEN OFF PROBATION FOR A WEEK NOW. MAYBE...

MAYBE WHAT?

YOU GOING TO *SEE* HIM?

WHAT DO YOU THINK?

fizz

STUFF

I KNOW YOU'RE ANGRY ABOUT HIM KEEPING THINGS FROM YOU, BUT IT'S BEEN SIX MONTHS SINCE HYKOSIS, CLEO. YOU CAN'T AVOID TALKING TO HIM FOREVER.

YASIRO ACADEMY
PART OF PHARAOH YASIRO'S RESEARCH
AND MILITARY INITIATIVE OF DEFENSE
(AKA: P.Y.R.A.M.I.D.)

SHUFF

OH MY
RA!

40

AS ADMIRABLE AS YOUR READINESS TO ASSIGN BLAME IS, CLEOPATRA, YOU WERE SHOCKINGLY NOT CALLED BEFORE THE COUNCIL TODAY FOR ANY INSUBORDINATION.

WE WILL, HOWEVER, DISCUSS THIS MATTER WITH PROFESSOR JAVEL AT A LATER DATE.

DOCTOR THEORIS, PLEASE INFORM CLEOPATRA AND THE REST OF THE COUNCIL OF WHY WE ARE ALL HERE.

YES. WELL, IN SHORT, WE BELIEVE WE'VE DISCOVERED THE RESTING PLACE OF THE GOLDEN LION.

A TEAM SHOULD BE PUT TOGETHER TO INSPECT THE SITE. TO BE SURE THE GOLDEN LION IS ON CADA'DUUN AND INTERCEPT OCTAVIAN IF HE IS INDEED AFTER IT.

AGREED.

GREAT!

WHEN DO WE LEAVE?

THAT SCHEDULE WILL BE DETERMINED BY ADMIRAL HASILRIG. *YOU*, ON THE OTHER HAND, ARE STILL GROUNDED.

GROUNDED?!

YES, FROM YOUR LITTLE OFF-BOOK FIELD TRIP TO HYKOSIS. OR MAYBE YOU FORGOT HOW YOUR RECKLESSNESS CAUSED THE DEATH OF ONE STUDENT AND PERMANENTLY INJURED ANOTHER.

BUT YOU'RE THE ONE WHO--

46

I'M THE ONE WHO **WHAT**?

EXCUSE ME, ADMINISTRANT KHEPRA, BUT IF CLEO IS NOT ALLOWED ON THE MISSION, WHY DID YOU CALL US IN HERE?

WE AGREED TO BE FORTHRIGHT WITH CLEOPATRA--

AND SINCE THIS NEWS OF THE GOLDEN LION INVOLVES THE TABLETS--

WAIT-- **TABLETS?**

YES, ASIDE FROM THE SCROLL CADET THEORIS QUOTED EARLIER, THE GOLDEN LION IS ALSO REFERRED TO ON THE UTA TABLET.

YOU DID **READ** THE UTA TABLET WHEN YOU STUMBLED UPON IT LAST YEAR, DIDN'T YOU?

UM...

WHAT KIND OF CONDITIONS ARE THOSE?

IN A WORD: SNOW.

I LOVE SNOW!

AT LEAST, I *THINK* I'D LOVE IT.

NOT THIS KIND, CLEO.

I BELIEVE THAT CONCLUDES THESE MATTERS.

UNLESS THERE ARE ANY MORE QUESTIONS?

VERY WELL, THEN.

COUNCIL DISMISSED.

ONCE AGAIN, SOME ANCIENT SOMETHING-OR-OTHER THAT'S RELATED TO WHY I'M HERE SURFACES, AND I CAN'T DO ANYTHING ABOUT IT.

MUST BE A TUESDAY.

WHAT'S UP WITH THIS COUNCIL? DO THEY WANT YOUR HELP SAVING THE GALAXY OR WHAT?

AT LEAST THEY KEPT YOU INFORMED OF WHAT'S GOING ON THIS TIME. THAT'S PRETTY TRUSTING.

YEAH, I GUESS.

KHENSU COULD HAVE AT LEAST STUCK UP FOR ME IN THERE, THOUGH.

CAN'T DEAL WITH SNOW.

WHAT AM I? FOUR YEARS OLD?

OH, KHEPRA HAS ALWAYS BEEN A BIT OF A STICK-IN-THE-MUD, EVEN WHEN SHE WAS A PROFESSOR HERE AT YASIRO ACADEMY.

NOT SURPRISED TO FIND HER SON FOLLOWING SUIT.

SON?!

KHEPRA IS KHENSU'S MOTHER. YOU DIDN'T KNOW THAT?

NO!

CLEOPATRA!

WE ARE GOING TO GRAB SOME LUNCH. WON'T YOU JOIN US?

I WOULD LOVE TO HEAR ABOUT YOUR TIME ON EARTH. SPECIFICALLY, IF OUR RESEARCH CORRELATES WITH YOUR LIFE IN EGYPT AND YOUR THOUGHTS ON GOVERNMENTAL PRACTICES DURING THE PTOLEMAIC ERA.

UM...THAT SOUNDS...

APOLOGIES, DOCTOR THEORIS, BUT I'M GOING TO HAVE TO STEAL CLEOPATRA FROM YOU.

OH.

OKAY.

SORRY, GUYS!

ENJOY YOUR TIME WITH YOUR PARENTS, KI KI.

PLEASE DON'T CALL ME THAT.

NOPE!

YOU'RE KI KI NOW.

KHEPRA BELIEVES SHE SPEAKS FOR ALL OF US.

THERE ARE SOME MEMBERS OF THE COUNCIL WHO TAKE THE PROPHECIES MORE SERIOUSLY THAN SHE DOES.

THERE IS GREAT INTELLIGENCE IN YOU, CLEOPATRA, WHETHER YOU CHOOSE TO RECOGNIZE IT OR NOT.

I HAVE THE UTMOST CONFIDENCE THAT YOU WILL KNOW WHAT TO DO WITH THAT.

OR FIND SOMEONE WHO DOES.

I HATE THAT EXCUSE.

HEY, YOU AND ME BOTH!

I CAN PROBABLY INSTALL IT IN YOUR BIKE, BUT...

LOOK...

CADA'DUUN ISN'T THE KIND OF PLACE YOU SHOULD GO TO ALONE.

THAT'S WHAT YOU SAID ABOUT HYKOSIS AND I GOT BACK OKAY.

YOU CAME BACK IN A *COMA*.

AND SOME OF US...

PRECISELY.

I DON'T WANT ANYONE ELSE RISKING THEIR LIFE FOR MATTERS THAT CONCERN ME OR ANY OF THE TWELVE MILLION PROPHECIES OUT THERE **ABOUT** ME.

IT'S NOT A GOOD IDEA, CLEO.

BESIDES...

I HEARD YOU'RE GROUNDED.

EH...IT'S A FLEXIBLE SORT OF GROUNDED.

C'MON, BRIAN. WHY WOULD KEK GIVE THAT TO ME IF HE DIDN'T WANT ME TO USE IT?

MAYBE THERE'S A REASON I'M SUPPOSED TO GO ALONE.

IT'S NOT JUST THAT. THE ENVIRONMENTAL CONDITIONS IN THAT SECTION OF THE GALAXY ARE INCREDIBLY HARSH.

I'M NOT SURE EVEN A *SAVIOR OF THE GALAXY* IS EQUIPPED TO HANDLE THEM.

THEN EQUIP ME.

IF I DON'T HELP YOU WITH THIS, YOU'RE PROBABLY GOING TO TRY TO FIND A WAY OUT THERE ON YOUR OWN, AREN'T YOU?

PROBABLY.

AND IT'LL INVOLVE A METHOD THAT WILL MOST LIKELY GET YOU KILLED, WON'T IT?

MOST LIKELY.

UGH.

FINE.

YAY!

THANKS, BRIAN!

YOU'RE NOT GONNA TELL ANYONE ABOUT THIS, ARE YOU?

ABOUT YOU HUGGING ME?

WHAT? NO! ME GOING OFF TO *CADA'DUUN.*

ALONE.

UM...

OF COURSE NOT.

YOU *CAN'T* TELL KI KI--I MEAN AKILA--BRIAN. SHE'LL JUST TRY TO TALK ME OUT OF IT. OR WORSE, WANT TO HELP.

YEAH, YEAH. OKAY.

BUT SINCE *I'M* ALREADY HELPING YOU...

YOU'RE NOT COMING WITH ME EITHER, BRIAN.

THAT'S NOT-- I WOULDN'T GO TO CADA'DUUN IF IT WAS THE LAST PLACE TO FIND COMPUTER PARTS.

WHAT I MEAN IS, YOU'RE GOING TO NEED MORE THAN JUST A CHEETAH CELL UPGRADE.

OKAY. LIKE WHAT?

FOR STARTERS...

CLEO!

CLEO!

A-ANTONY?

HERE. EAT THIS.

IT'LL WARM YOU UP.

munch

gulp

munch munch

FIRE FRUIT. IT SHOULD KEEP YOU WARM FOR AT LEAST A DAY OR TWO.

WELL, **WARMER**, AT LEAST.

munch munch

YOU'RE LUCKY THAT WAS ONLY A **BABY** ICE SPIDER.

IT WAS JUST PLAYING WITH YOU.

PLAYING...?

WHAT ARE YOU **DOING** HERE, ANTONY?

SAME THING YOU ARE, I IMAGINE.

HERE FOR THE GOLDEN LION, AREN'T YOU?

HOW DO YOU KNOW ABOUT THE GOLDEN LION?

EVERYONE KNOWS ABOUT THE GOLDEN LION. LEGENDARY STAR. IMMEASURABLE SOURCE OF POWER.

THERE ARE QUITE A LOT OF PEOPLE OUT THERE WHO WILL PAY SOME HANDSOME CREDITS FOR JUST A PIECE OF IT.

WELL, THOSE WHO ACTUALLY BELIEVE IN IT, ANYWAY.

THEN OCTAVIAN DEFINITELY KNOWS ABOUT IT...

HUH?

WAIT--SO THAT'S WHY YOU'RE HERE? YOU'RE LOOKING TO COLLECT A BOUNTY ON THE GOLDEN LION?

THIS TREASURE HUNTER'S GOTTA EAT.

SO YOU WILL SELL A POTENTIALLY DANGEROUS WEAPON JUST TO MAKE A FEW BUCKS!

HEY! LIGHT FUEL ISN'T CHEAP!

BOOP

VRACK VRACK

AT LEAST THIS STILL WORKS.

BLOOP

YEAH, I DON'T KNOW IF IT'S JUST THE COLD OR SOMETHING ELSE TO DO WITH THE ATMOSPHERE ON THIS PLANET, BUT IT'S NOT VERY INVITING TO TECHNOLOGY.

MY ENERGY SPHERES BARELY HAD ENOUGH JUICE TO SCARE AWAY THE ICE SPIDER.

DOES YOUR SHIP STILL WORK?

YOURS DOESN'T?

CHAPTER TWO

OKAY-- WHO **WAS** THAT OUT THERE?

MUST HAVE BEEN ANOTHER BOUNTY HUNTER. WHEN A TREASURE AS LARGE AS THE GOLDEN LION IS DISCOVERED, WORD SPREADS QUICKLY.

SHHUFF

WE SHOULD BE SAFE IN HERE FOR NOW, AT LEAST.

THANK RA FOR YOUR, UH... GLOWING.

AGAIN.

YOU'RE CRAZY.

YOU SEE A LOT OF CRAZY STUFF TRAVERSING THE COSMOS. I DON'T DISCOUNT ANYTHING THESE DAYS.

WELL, IT'S STILL WEIRD.

YEAH. IT IS.

SHIVER

BACK HOME...

MY **OLD** HOME, ON EARTH...

I USED TO STARE UP AT THEM EVERY NIGHT.

WHEN I WAS YOUNGER, MY MOTHER USED TO TELL ME THEY WERE THE SOULS OF OUR **ANCESTORS.** THERE WAS SOMETHING COMFORTING IN THE THOUGHT THAT EVEN THOUGH IT TOOK DEATH TO GET THEM THERE, THEY HAD ESCAPED THE CONFINES OF THEIR RESPONSIBILITIES.

THEY FINALLY HAD A WHOLE NIGHT SKY TO PLAY AND EXPLORE IN.

THE CONSTELLATIONS ARE DIFFERENT NOW, BUT STILL...

I DIDN'T EVEN KNOW WHAT A GALAXY **WAS** A YEAR AGO.

AM I GLOWING AGAIN?

NO, NO!

IT'S JUST--

toss

IF YOU'RE SO DOWN ON BEING RESPONSIBLE, WHY DO YOU STILL WEAR THAT CROWN?

HUH?

I'VE NEVER SEEN YOU WITHOUT IT, EVEN WHEN IT COULD HAVE CAUSED YOU TROUBLE ON HYKOSIS.

I DUNNO.

IT'S A FAMILY HEIRLOOM.

IT'S...ALL I HAVE LEFT.

HEH.

I NEVER THOUGHT ABOUT IT TILL NOW, BUT THE IBIS ON IT--

IT'S A TYPE OF BIRD ON EARTH.

THE IBIS IS THE SHAPE THOTH OFTEN TOOK IN THE STORIES MY MOM TOLD ME, AND NOW HE'S SUPPOSEDLY THE ONE WHO GOT ME IN THIS MESS.

THAT'S A BIRD?

YEAH?

I THOUGHT IT WAS A SNAKE.

WHAT?

IT'S **TOTALLY** A BIRD!

LOOKS LIKE A SNAKE.

ARE YOU KIDDING ME?

WE NEED TO STAY WARM.

WAIT.

YOU AREN'T TRYING TO EAT ME, ARE YOU?

CHIRP

HEY!

CHIRP! CHIRP!

YOU WANT ME TO FOLLOW YOU?

CHIRP!

Z

ALL RIGHT.

CHIRP!

YUP.

IT'S A TOMB.

THERE YOU--

WHOA.

HOW'D YOU KNOW THIS WAS HERE?

MIHOS LED ME TO IT.

MIHOS?

CHIRP!

A SNOW OTTER?

THEY AREN'T DANGEROUS, ARE THEY?

NOT THAT I'VE HEARD OF.

Sniff

GOOD. I'VE NAMED HER MIHOS.

HIM.

HUH?

SHE'S A HE.

THE FEMALES HAVE SPOTTED TAILS.

CHIRP!

ANYWAY, WE SHOULD TURN BACK.

WHAT? WE SHOULD GO THROUGH THIS DOOR!

NO WAY. EVERY TIME I ENTER A DOOR IN SOME MYSTERIOUS TOMB, SOMETHING TERRIBLE HAPPENS.

LET'S TRY TO CLIMB UP TO THAT OPENING BACK AT THE ENTRANCE.

DON'T BE SILLY. THIS DOOR COULD LEAD US TO SOMETHING...

LIKE...

LIKE TREASURE?

DON'T START.

I WAS GONNA SAY CLUES TO THE GOLDEN LION.

HERE.
THESE LOOK
LIKE BUTTONS.
AND...

THESE LOOK
LIKE...

ALGEBRAIC
EQUATIONS.

YOU'RE
KIDDING
ME.

WHY? YOU
GOOD AT
MATH?

NOT
REALLY.

THERE'S GOTTA BE...

GREAT.

WE'RE TRAPPED WORSE THAN BEFORE.

CLACK

UH...

AH!

YAH!

CHIRP!

CHUNK

oOOOh

CHIRP

AT LEAST WE LANDED ON SOMETHING SOFT.

IT'S... MOSS.

HEY-- ARE YOU **WARM**?

HEY! YEAH, I'M ACTU--

OH!

WHOA!

CHIRP!

CHAPTER THREE

DRIP

DRIP

FOOD AIN'T BAD, EITHER.

CHIRP!

HMM?

HEE HEE HEE HEE

HEY!

CLEO!

I THINK I'M STARTING TO GET AHOLD OF THE LANGUAGE IN THIS CITY.

IT'S ACTUALLY NOT TOO TOUGH TO FIGURE OUT IF YOU KNOW A LITTLE RUDIMENTARY ALGEBRA.

HEE HEE HEE

WHAT DID YOU SAY TO THEM?

YOU WOULDN'T GET IT.

CADA'DUUNIAN HUMOR.

HEE HEE HEE

THAT'S NOT ALL.

CHECK IT OUT.

MY BIKE!

AND MY SHIP.

THEY OFFERED TO LOCATE AND RETRIEVE THEM FOR US.

I KNOW IT MIGHT NOT SEEM LIKE IT AT FIRST, BUT THESE PEOPLE ARE PRETTY ADVANCED. THEY EVEN HAVE SHIPS THAT CAN TRAVEL IN THE ATMOSPHERE UP ABOVE-- AS LONG AS THEY DON'T RUN INTO ANY OF THOSE SNOWSTORMS WE ENCOUNTERED.

OH, THIS IS RIDICULOUS.

ANYWAY, WE ARE INVITED TO A DINNER TONIGHT WITH THE CHIEF OF THIS PLACE.

I WAS THINKING IT COULD BE A GOOD OPPORTUNITY TO BRING UP...

YOU KNOW...

THE *STAR*.

POKE

?

BEEP
BEEP
BEEP

BLOOP
BLOOP

OUR SENSORS ARE WORKING AGAIN!

BEEP
BEEP

BEEP

ヽ∵乙田(ಠ_ಠ)ヽ
√(凸)Ⅲ〜(∅)?

nod

C'MON.

WAIT!

MIHOS...

THE WHOLE CITY IS OVERRUN.

HOW DID THOSE CHROME TOPS EVEN FIND THIS--

HEY--

DᵣᵤⱣ!

IT'S THAT BOUNTY HUNTER!

HE'S AFTER THE GOLDEN LION.

WE CAN'T LET HIM NEAR IT.

IF HE DESTROYS IT, IT WILL DEVASTATE THIS ENTIRE AREA.

DESTROY? WHY WOULD HE--

C'MON!

VRACK
VRACK

ZWACK
ZWACK
ZWACK

ZWIP

THUNK
THUNK

OH.

I JUST THOUGHT WITH--

WAIT.

WEREN'T YOU...?

CHIRP!

CHIRP!

MIHOS!

Oof!

SHOVE

YOU'RE OKAY.

YOU DID SO GOOD.

GOOD ATTACK OTTER!

CHIRP!

AT LEAST ONE OF US GETS SOME GRATITUDE.

BRIAN?

WHAT ARE YOU DOING HERE?

HOW DID YOU EVEN **FIND** THIS PLACE?

AND **WHY** DO I NOT HAVE MY OWN JETPACK?

FWISH

I PLACED A BEACON IN YOUR BIKE WHEN I UPGRADED IT.

AND NO ONE TRUSTS YOU WITH A JETPACK, CLEO.

FOR A WHILE I THOUGHT THE BEACON WASN'T WORKING PROPERLY. THEN, AN HOUR AGO WE NOTICED A SIGNAL. WE'VE BEEN HOVERING ABOVE THE PLANET TRYING TO DETECT THE GOLDEN LION FOR A COUPLE DAYS NOW, BUT OUR ENERGY SENSORS HAD A DIFFICULT TIME FUNCTIONING THROUGH THE ATMOSPHERE.

YEAH, TELL ME ABOUT IT.

IT'S CLEAR NOW THAT THIS CAVERN IS SOMEHOW IMMUNE TO ANY ELECTRONIC INTERFERENCE.

I'D LOVE TO TALK TO SOME OF THE SCIENTISTS HERE.

HA-- GOOD LUCK WITH THAT.

ON SECOND THOUGHT, **YOU'D** PROBABLY HAVE NO PROBLEM.

CLEO!

WHAT WERE YOU **THINKING**?

SIMPLE.

SHE WASN'T.

HEY! HOLD ON--

WHY ARE YOU ALL HERE?

I TOLD AKILA.

I TOLD KHENSU.

I TOLD EVERYONE ELSE.

SERIOUSLY, CLEO. AFTER HYKOSIS, I THOUGHT YOU WOULD HAVE KNOWN BETTER THAN TO RUN OFF TO A FAR-REACHING, INHOSPITABLE PLANET BY YOURSELF.

AND YOU'D THINK AFTER A YEAR NOW, KHENSU WOULD KNOW CLEO BETTER THAN THAT.

I KNOW.

YOU'RE RIGHT.

AND ANOTHER THI--

...

SAY AGAIN?

YOU WERE **RIGHT.** I SHOULDN'T HAVE COME HERE ON MY OWN. I DIDN'T WANT ANYONE RISKING THEIR LIFE FOR MY SAKE, BUT I REALIZE NOW THAT I'M RISKING MY **OWN** LIFE IF I DON'T ACCEPT HELP. AND IF I REALLY AM THE ONE DESTINED TO DEFEAT OCTAVIAN, THAT'S NOT FAIR TO ANYONE. IT WAS SELFISH AND IRRESPONSIBLE, AND I'M SORRY.

ALSO, I'M GOING TO START PAYING BETTER ATTENTION IN ALGEBRA CLASS.

CHIRP!

HE'S **ADORABLE!**

WOW, A SNOW OTTER. THOSE ARE SUPER RARE.

SUPPOSEDLY REALLY SMART, TOO.

YEAH, IF IT WASN'T FOR MIHOS HERE, ANTONY AND I MIGHT NOT HAVE--

WAIT--

ANTONY'S HERE?

YEAH, HE WAS JUST...

UM...

I'LL BE RIGHT BACK.

I THOUGHT SHE SAID SHE WASN'T GOING TO RUN OFF ALONE AGAIN.

TOO CROWDED FOR YOU?

I'VE FOUND IT WISE NOT TO STICK AROUND A PLACE TOO LONG ONCE P.Y.R.A.M.I.D. GETS INVOLVED.

BESIDES, LOOKS LIKE THEY'VE GOT THINGS COVERED HERE.

YOU COULD COME BACK TO YASIRO ACADEMY WITH ME. P.Y.R.A.M.I.D. WOULD PROBABLY LOVE TO HAVE SOMEONE WITH YOUR TALENTS.

P.Y.R.A.M.I.D. WOULD PROBABLY **ARREST** ME.

VSSSCH

IT'S A **BIRD!**

SEE, MIHOS...

PLENTY OF ZUTUPPLE FRUIT FOR THE TRIP BACK TO MAYET.

CHIRP CHIRP!

MIHOS!

CHIRP

HEY--YOU'RE MY PET!

HE'S NOT A *PET*, CLEO. HE'S FULLY CAPABLE OF DECIDING WHO'S THE BETTER CUDDLER.

ISN'T THAT RIGHT, MIHOS.

WELL, I NAMED HIM...

I CAN'T WAIT TO PLAY WITH SOME OF THIS TECH ONCE WE GET BACK TO YASIRO ACADEMY. THE CADA'DUUNIANS HAVE SUCH A UNIQUE WAY OF LOOKING AT THINGS.

ORGANICS AND NATURE COMPLETELY INTERTWINED WITH TECHNOLOGY.

P.Y.R.A.M.I.D. WILL LEARN A LOT FROM THEM.

YOUR PARENTS ARE STILL INTENT ON STAYING HERE, THEN?

YEAH. NOT ONLY WAS THIS BASIN A GREAT ARCHAEOLOGICAL FIND, BUT THE GOLDEN LION IS HERE, TOO.

OBVIOUSLY WE CAN'T MOVE IT, SO THEY ARE GOING TO STUDY IT HERE.

IT'LL BE GOOD TO HAVE A FEW P.Y.R.A.M.I.D. SOLDIERS STATIONED IN THE CITY AS WELL IN CASE THERE'S ANOTHER XERX ATTACK ON THE PLACE.

I CAN'T IMAGINE WHAT OCTAVIAN WOULD DO IF HE GOT HOLD OF THAT SORT OF POWER.

I'M SORRY, AKILA. YOU HAVEN'T SEEN YOUR PARENTS IN FOREVER, AND NOW THEY'RE LEAVING AGAIN.

THEY ACTUALLY ASKED IF I WANTED TO STAY, BUT I STILL HAVE A LOT TO LEARN AT THE ACADEMY.

Sniff

I'LL MISS THEM, BUT I HONESTLY FORGOT HOW CONTROLLING THEY ARE. I THINK I GOT KIND OF USED TO HAVING SOME FREEDOM.

BESIDES, AS GREAT AS THESE CADA'DUUNIANS ARE, I'M NOT SURE I CAN ONLY SPEAK IN ALGEBRAIC EQUATIONS FOR AS LONG AS I'M HERE.

THANK YOU!

AHEM.

UM...WE'LL LEAVE YOU TWO ALONE.

C'MON, MIHOS!

LOOK, KHENSU... I...

I'M PROUD OF YOU, CLEO.

KHENSU!

CHIEF WANTS A WORD BEFORE WE TAKE OFF.

WE GOOD?

WE'RE GOOD.

NO MORE LIES?

NO MORE LIES.

SO YOU RETRIEVED WHAT I WANTED?

DEPENDS.

YOUR PRECIOUS ORPHANAGE IS SAFE.

THE BOUNTY ON ME. I ALSO WANT THAT LIFTED.

BLOOP

DONE.

DON'T MAKE ME REGRET THIS ARRANGEMENT ANY FURTHER.

TOSS

CATCH

SPECIAL THANKS TO:

My extraordinarily encouraging wife, Jen, whose patience and selflessness know no bounds.

My two boys, Oliver and Orion. I hope you enjoy these books one day. Also, please stop chasing the cat.

My cat, Misty, for putting up with Oliver and Orion while I was too busy working to save you.

The rest of my *incredibly* supportive friends and family. I am blessed to have so many of you in my life.

Cassandra Pelham and David Saylor for keeping this series steering in the right direction, Phil Falco for making it look so good, and Lizette Serrano, Sheila Marie Everett, Tracy van Straaten, Michelle Campbell, Antonio Gonzalez, Denise Anderson, Ed Masessa, and all the other wonderful folks at Scholastic for the amazing work you've put into it.

Judy Hansen, for your super heroics.

Dan Conner and Kate Carleton for once again helping to make sure this book got colored on time.

Christ, for Your guidance and the freedom to accept or ignore it.

And last but not least, the Internet, for the music and company.

EXTRA SPECIAL THANKS TO:

All of the teachers, librarians, booksellers, parents, and readers out there who have supported Cleopatra in Space and/or given me high fives. CONTINUE TO BE AWESOME!

ABOUT THE AUTHOR

A graduate of the Columbus College of Art & Design, Mike Maihack spends his time drawing comics and making sure his house doesn't collapse from the chaos that ensues from two boys bouncing around inside of it. He's contributed to several books, including Sensation Comics Featuring Wonder Woman; *Parable*; *Jim Henson's The Storyteller*; Cow Boy; *Geeks, Girls, and Secret Identities*; and *Comic Book Tattoo*. *The Golden Lion* is the fourth graphic novel in the Cleopatra in Space series, following the Florida Book Award–winning *Target Practice*, *The Thief and the Sword*, and *Secret of the Time Tablets*. He lives in the almost-tropical climate of Lutz, Florida, and is thankful that math isn't required to communicate with the locals.

Visit Mike online at www.mikemaihack.com and follow him on Twitter at @mikemaihack.